I0553701

SUNSHINE

ALYSE ZAFTIG

ZAFTIG PUBLISHING

CONTENTS

1 / BIRTH
HUDSON

"IT'S A BOY."

I looked at the squalling baby in front of me. He was covered in various bodily fluids. The doctor briskly spanked him. He screamed.

"Strong lungs." He kept checking him. "Apgar score of six." A nurse took him away to give him his first bath.

My lovely but sweaty wife was glad, and she was exhausted. Her eyes were closed as the nurse kept cleaning her up.

"It's our baby. I'm so glad to meet him. Baby Chris." I moved up and took my wife's hand.

The nurse nodded. "I'll put it on the birth

certificate. Isabel King and Hudson King as the parents. Chris King as the baby. What's his middle name?"

"Adam, after my father." My wife's voice was so faint. The nurse filled out the form and walked off.

"I'm so glad you're healthy, and he's here."

I squeezed her hand.

"We have a problem."

I whipped around to look at the nurse who was talking to my wife's OBGYN. "What's going on?" There was a note of panic in my voice. I forced myself to be calm. "What's going on?"

"She won't stop bleeding."

"I thought that it was normal to have all this." I gestured at the fluids.

"Yes, but her placenta merged with her uterus, and she won't stop bleeding. She's hemorrhaging out. We're going to have to take her into surgery. We need to do a hysterectomy."

"Baby," my wife said, her hand weak in mine. "I'll be fine. Just let the doctors do their job."

The nurse and doctor undid the brakes of the bed, and they wheeled her into the maternity ward operating room. They wouldn't let me in there.

I went to the nursery to look at my son. He was small. He was in one of those clear cribs, and I could see that he was bigger than the other babies. He was wailing, and I already knew that he was going to be a troublemaker and a handful to raise. I smiled. I relished the challenge, as long as my wife was right there beside me.

I watched the clock tick, but nobody came out of the OR. I got more and more tense as first one hour then two dragged by.

An alarm went off. I watched as all the nurses on the unit filed into the OR.

"She's coding!"

I stood with my back against the wall, waiting for more news. What did coding mean? Was there something going wrong in the OR?

I stood watch at the doors. My wife's OBGYN, Dr. Lawson, came out. He was covered in blood. It covered all of his scrubs.

"I'm sorry, Mr. King. We lost her."

My whole body went numb.

"No. This is a hospital. You can save her here."

"I'm sorry, sir. Yes. She's dead."

"But the baby..."

The doctor took off his gloves and shook his head. "You're going to have to take care of him yourself. I can call the chaplain if you want."

"I'm not religious."

"He's here for spiritual guidance more than religious guidance."

"No thank you." I shook my head. "How long can I leave my son here?" I had no idea how to take care of a baby.

The doctor frowned. "We normally keep the baby until the mother is ready to be discharged. But we can keep the baby for up to 5 days, unless they need to be in the NICU."

"Okay. Bye."

The doctor ran after me. "Don't you want to hold your son?"

I looked at him. I looked at my hands, which were shaking. I would drop the baby. "No."

The doctor's jaw dropped.

I turned and walked out of the maternity ward, leaving my son behind.

2 / PHONE CALLS
HUDSON

I WENT home and took a shower. I washed off the sick scent of the hospital. I stood there in the shower, with the steam rising around me. My wife was dead. I had to arrange a funeral.

I hadn't gotten to say goodbye. She was gone, just like that, on what should have been the happiest day of our lives after our wedding day. She had never held our son.

I felt the wetness on my cheeks. I pretended it was the shower. What was I going to do?

I had my own company focused on small enterprise IT solutions, with a focus on security systems. I helped new businesses get started from soup to nuts, with all the software that they needed on the backend. I worked more than 100 hours a week.

I regretted the time that took me away from my wife. All those hours and days that I should have been by her side, soaking her up like a sponge. She was too young to die like this.

I pounded my fist against the wet, unforgivingly cold tile. It wasn't supposed to be like this. This was the furthest thing from fair.

I had to arrange her funeral. I had to get a nanny for my newborn. I didn't have time for the business that had eaten my life and stolen what I should have given to my wife.

I sat down at my computer. First, I fired off a phone call to my lawyer asking him to look for potential acquirers for my business. His secretary said that he would get back to me. Second, I looked through the Yellow Pages to look for funeral homes. I chose one that looked like it would be big enough. I'd heard its name before. They said that they'd set up a funeral for 2 days from now. Third, I called a nanny service.

"Hello. How can we help you today?"

"Hi. My name is Hudson King. I need a nanny."

"Excellent. We can help you. What kind of nanny do you need?"

"My wife just died."

I heard an intake of breath on the other side. "Oh. I'm so sorry."

"My baby was born a few hours ago."

Another gasp.

"I need someone who can take care of a newborn. Someone who knows what they are doing and can come on short notice."

"Well, sir, there's only one person available. Jalanda is the newest nanny to join us. She has impeccable references. She worked in Italy for the past two years, taking care of a pair of twins. She's the best we can do."

"I'll take her."

"But sir, you don't even know how much she costs."

"I'll take her. I don't care how much it costs." I'd be rolling in money soon anyway. I didn't care about the cash. Any problem that could be solved with money was not a problem. "Just send her to my place as soon as possible. Then we can get my son." I hung up the phone.

I ran my hand through my buzz cut. I just had to do the best I could.

3 / FUNERAL
HUDSON

I WAS dry-eyed through the funeral. Everyone who had come to our wedding only a year before was there, somber and wearing black.I stood there, numb, as the eulogy went on and on. They'd wanted me to say it. What could I say about her? That she was stolen too young? That she was my wife? Now she was gone. Chris wasn't at the funeral. The nanny had him.

I endured as person after person shook my hand and told me how sorry they were during the wake. My mother was there. While she normally had very little pity for wallowing, she could tell that this time was different. She handled the details of the funeral, shielding me from the worst of my grief.

My life stretched in front of me like an endless night. There was no point in anything. My wife was dead. I had a baby that I didn't want to see. I knew it wasn't fair, but the baby had stolen away my wife. I was ashamed, but I'd rather have my wife than a dozen babies. I loved her. I had loved her since we were kids. And now she was dead. Gone.

I was in my mother's car as she drove the two of us into the cemetery. Isabel was wrapped in an expensive mahogany box. In a few years, she would decay under the ground, becoming part of the soil.

We didn't have many people at the cemetery. Most people were asked just to go to the funeral. It was my mom, her parents, and me at the grave as they lowered my wife into the cold dirt. Tears streamed down my face as they filled in the dirt on top of her. She was gone. Really gone.

I got back into the car. I noticed that there was grass on my shoes. I didn't care. I practically bought out the nearest shoe store when it came to black polish, but my shoes didn't matter now. Nothing did.

My mother drove me home.

"I want to meet my grandson."

I got out of the car and unlocked my front door.

My mother walked in behind me.

"Where is he?"

I walked towards the nursery. The nanny was in there, singing softly to the baby. My son was sleeping in his blue crib.

"What a little angel." My mom touched his fuzzy baby head. "He is so beautiful."

I looked at him. He looked so much like Isabel. It hurt. His face was chubby, unlike hers, but he looked so much like her. It was Isabel was there, living in her son. My heart felt like someone had plunged a knife in it.

My mom said, "We should go. We don't want to wake up the baby."

I followed her out of the nursery. She looked through an open door. "Who else is living with you?"

"The nanny lives here."

"That is good. You need the help."

I knew that I needed it, but my mom telling me that I needed it rankled.

"Don't you have a plane to catch?"

She looked at her watch. "Yes, I do. I will come back."

I hoped that she would not. "Okay."

I watched as she drove away. I closed my front door, shutting out the rest of the world.

I walked into my office and shut the door. I took out a bottle of bourbon. I drank straight from the bottle. This is going to be my constant companion now that Isabel was gone.

4 / DINNER
JALANDA

I TUCKED his little body around a pillow. He was so precious like this. His soft skin and the sweet smell of his head were the best parts of my job.

I checked my watch. It was getting late. I had not had dinner.

I knocked on the office door. I waited for a moment.

"Yes?"

"I was wondering if you wanted dinner."

The door opened. "Dinner sounds nice."

"How about some pepperoni pizza?"

"Sounds good to me." He picked up some of our junk mail. "I can call them."

After 30 minutes, a delivery guy came to our door. Mr. King paid the pizza delivery guy in cash, and he sent him on his way.

The two of us ate our pizza in silence at the table. We did not use plates. We just used napkins. I was not in the mood to wash dishes.

"Can I get you a drink?"

"What do you have?"

"Well, I normally drink some wine with dinner."

"Wine sounds good to me."

He poured us two glasses of wine.

"To life!" He drank his entire glass.

I took a sip of my wine. "This is good. What is it?"

"Bordeaux. You like?"

"I love it."

"I have a feeling that we're going to be consuming a lot of alcohol in this household."

I cleared my throat. "We should talk."

"Yeah?"

"I need to buy stuff for the baby. He has a crib, but he needs more clothes."

"We did not know the gender of the baby. We wanted it to be a surprise."

"Yeah."

"I will give you a credit card. Just go ahead and use it for whatever you think he needs."

I nodded. "Do you want me to do the grocery shopping?"

"That would be nice." He poured more wine into his glass. "I have a cleaning service that comes once a week. Can you cook?"

"Yeah. I mean, I am not a gourmet chef. However, I can do basic cooking. I learned a lot in Italy."

"Italy. I have never been there."

He drank more wine. "Like I said, I have that cleaning service that comes once a week, so I'm definitely set for that. So just some basic cooking or ordering in some food will be fine. Just get some meals on the table, whether you are cooking them or not."

"What do you like?"

"Anything, honestly. My parents exposed me to so many weird foods when I was a kid that I don't really care what I eat." He shrugged, and I tried not to notice how delicious his broad shoulders were.

"So some basic Italian would be fine? I'll order in some nights, for variety, but I can whip up some quick pasta if we just want to take it easy at home."

"Yeah, that would be great." He drained his glass. "I have to go." He wandered off upstairs, probably to his suite.

I finished up my wine and pizza, and I cleaned up the table. It soothed me to clear the crumbs off and leave the surface clean again.

5 / *BUSYBODY*
HUDSON

MY MOTHER only left me alone for a week. I sold my business hastily, leaving some money on the table if they promised that I could walk away and not help them transition. I was in no shape to do it, anyways. I should have known that my mother couldn't leave me alone.

She swept back into my house after she stepped out of the black car. She had her own room. Not because I'd given it to her, though. She'd just camped out in one of my bedrooms, leaving her stuff in there. My house was so uselessly large that it didn't matter. I tried not to get involved in any conflict with my mother if I could avoid it.

"Have you even left this house over the past week?"

"No." I wasn't going to lie. She was my mother. She could see it on my face and hear it in my voice. She was uncanny.

"You need to. You're going to waste away back here."

"Mom, my wife has been buried under the ground for a week. I need a little more time to grieve."

She sniffed. "If I leave you alone, then you'll wallow."

"Mom, my wife just died. Most people would let me wallow."

"You know that I've never believed in that kind of thing."

I didn't roll my eyes. She had spanked me as a kid for it, and she wasn't afraid to do it now.

"Yeah, Mom, I know."

"You have a date tonight."

"Mom! My wife is barely cold! This is inappropriately fast."

"What, do you want to sit in your house wearing

funeral colors every day for the first three years of your son's life?"

"Well..." That did sound pretty attractive, frankly.

"No! I won't allow it. You're going to get out there and live again. None of this moping around. You know that Isabel wouldn't have wanted it."

I sniffed, but not because there were tears in my eyes. No. Men did not cry. "I don't want to date anybody tonight."

"You're going." Her tone brooked no argument. "You're too young to waste away. Look at me. Your father was done, and I was already getting cards from gentlemen callers at his funeral."

"Mom. Seriously inappropriate."

"I bought you a new Zegna suit for it."

"Mom! Honestly! Too much."

"I'm not going to watch you die alongside your young wife. I know that it was sudden, but you owe it to your son not to be a formless, pale blob. Have you even spent any time with him?"

She could read my guilt from the way that I didn't meet her eyes.

"He has a nanny who loves him."

Mom came to point like a dog. "The girl I saw before?" She tapped her chin. "I should check on my grandson. Stay here."

I wasn't a dog that she could command to sit and stay. I followed her as she cracked open the door to my nursery room.

My nanny was holding my son in her arms, walking in a circle around the room, singing softly to him. I could see his tiny eyelids drooping as he slowly fell asleep.

We got out of the nursery.

"That girl does love him, little Chris. And a good thing, too, if his father neglects him."

I stared at my feet.

"Just as well. Is she going to be here to take care of the baby when you go on your date tonight?"

"Yeah. She's a live-in nanny."

"Great. You need to pick this woman up at this address." She handed me a perfumed calling card. I grimaced from the stink. "Don't be late."

I took it from her. I didn't want to put it in my pocket. I walked to my fridge, and I got one of Isabel's refrigerator magnets. She had hand-painted a bunch of little wooden flowers, and she had glued strong magnets on them after the paint dried. I felt a lump in my throat. It didn't seem real that my wife was even gone, and now I was using her magnet to affix a date with her replacement on my fridge. Our fridge.

I took it off of the fridge.

"Don't throw it out. You need this. You don't have to marry her. You just need to get out of the house."

Mom must have read my mind. I sighed. "Okay."

I PICKED her up from her place. Shoshanna was wearing a strapless red dress that was a little bit inappropriately short for a first date. It showcased her legs, though. It was fine.

I drove her to this small Mexican place I knew. It was quiet and intimate. They only had 10 tables, so you had to make a reservation about a month in advance to get in for lunch or dinner. It was my kind of style. Isabel and I had gone here every few months and fed each other the delicious guacamole that they gave everyone for appetizers alongside tortilla chips that they made fresh every day.

I knew that it wasn't the biggest place, but why not wear my heart on my sleeve? It wasn't like I was trying to impress her.

When we pulled into the gravel parking lot, I got out of the car. I walked around to open her door.

She looked down at the gravel. "I'm not walking on that."

I looked at her six-inch heels. "What do you want to do?"

"Let's go somewhere else."

I rapidly calculated. I'd lose this dinner reservation, and I probably wouldn't be here for another couple months. She was making me miss out on my guac and my chiles rellenos en nogada (in walnut sauce). I didn't say anything.

She looked at my face. "Oh, well, I mean, I guess we can stay here if you want."

"No, it's fine." I closed her door, and I walked back to my side. "Where do you want to go?"

"Let's go to Nobu."

I plugged it into my GPS, and we drove there. When we got in, the hostess told me that it would be a two-hour wait. I offered cash, but cash doesn't mean anything in LA. The hostess wrinkled her nose at me.

"The wait is two hours."

I turned to my date. "Do you want to go somewhere else?"

"No, let's stay here."

We stood in the crowded waiting area. When a seat opened up, we walked over so that she could sit down.

For another person, somebody warm and open like Isabel, this would have been an opportunity to get the date started and talk.

Instead, my date pulled a Harlequin romance out of her purse and began to read. I put my hands in my pockets. This was unbelievable. I wasn't hideous, and I had been out of the dating game since I got married. But surely it wasn't normal for people to read books on first dates?

I stared at the wall while she read her book, and I thought of all the ways that Isabel was better than this crazy girl. One, Isabel wouldn't sit down if I couldn't. I always offered, but she didn't want to ever be on unequal ground. Two, Isabel would never ignore me during a date like this. Three, Isabel would never, ever choose this restaurant over an intimate restaurant that I loved, even if she had never been in it before.

When we finally got a table, it felt like another 2 hours before a waiter came by to get our drink orders. I ordered salmon. She ordered some kind of Japanese salad.

She still wouldn't talk to me, even when we were seated at the same table. She just kept looking at her split ends.

I tried to make small talk. "So, uh, what do you do?"

"I work in marketing for Technicolor."

"Oh, yeah? That sounds interesting. What's that all about?"

She gave me a disgusted look. "It's exactly what it sounds like."

Okay, I guessed that I was shut down.

"What do you do?"

That was a good question. "Um, I'm not sure."

"You're not sure like you have a wide-reaching job description or you're not sure like you don't have a job?"

"Um, I guess I don't have a job. I'm sort of between things." I'd only just sold my first company for a few million, so I hadn't picked up the next thing yet. I had also spent all the time since my wife's death drinking and mourning the loss of our future.

She looked at me like I was a piece of filth on her shoe.

"Sorry, I just remembered that I have an early meeting tomorrow morning."

"What about the food?"

She stood up. "WAITER!" Our waiter came zooming in.

"Cancel our food order. We're leaving."

The entire restaurant was looking at us. A black man called from the back, "Looks like you done messed up, brother!"

I dropped a $100 bill on the table to thank the

waiter and pay for our drinks, and I followed her out.

She looked at my humble Taurus. "I should have known when you came to pick me up in this car. Oh my god, why do I date such losers?"

We got in the car, and I was elated as I drove her home. I didn't have to date anybody, especially not this psycho bitch. So we both got what we wanted. Who knew that posing as an unemployed guy would work so well?

As soon as I stopped in front of her house, she got out of my car. I was impressed by her speed in those super-high heels, because it looked like she was on stilts.

Her door slammed behind her. She hadn't said goodbye at all.

I whistled while I drove my car home. I thought I dodged a bullet there.

When I was home, the nanny had Chris in her arms. They were resting on a couch in front of the TV.

When she saw me, she jumped a little. Chris' eyes

opened blearily. He let out a trial cry. She patted his back and laid back on the couch. He nuzzled his face into her shoulder. She kissed his head.

I found myself abruptly a bit jealous of my own baby son. Isabel had always been affectionate. I didn't mean sexually, either. She put her hand on my arm when we talked. She put her arm around me sometimes. We held hands when we were sitting next to each other. I missed that. I missed her. And I missed touching anybody.

Maybe not telling the girl from tonight that I was a multimillionaire was a mistake. Oh well. There were plenty of fish in the sea.

How could I even think that? Isabel was my wife, and we were married forever. Until she died. And now my heart was broken in a million pieces.

"What are you doing home? I thought you'd be out tonight."

"It didn't go so well."

"Why are you smiling?"

"Because I don't have to go on any more dates."

7 / SECOND DATE
HUDSON

THE NEXT MORNING, I picked up the phone. I immediately wished that I had not.

"You told her that you didn't have a job!" my mom screamed.

"I didn't say that," I retorted. My voice was as smooth as silk. "She did."

"Oh my god, Hudson, what am I going to do with you? I find a nice, beautiful girl who looks like Isabel, and what do you do? You drive her off by telling her that you're unemployed. What did I buy that Zegna suit for anyway?"

For decorating the floor of my closet. "Sorry, Mom."

"Well." She paused. "I set up another date for you tonight."

"Mom, seriously, stop with the matchmaking. I have no interest in whatever poor girl you want to introduce to me."

"You're going, and that's that." She gave me an address, and I wrote it down on the white notepad that Isabel kept by the phone.

I picked up the next girl at a smaller house. She was very heavily made-up. She looked undead.

"Hi." I told her. "I'm Hudson."

"I know." She didn't introduce herself. She chewed her gum and blew a bubble. "So are we going to go out or what?"

"Where do you want to go?"

"How about Roscoe's Chicken and Waffles?"

Thank goodness she wasn't a stuck-up bitch like the first girl. "Okay."

We went in. We ordered fried chicken. I watched her annihilate a ton of chicken. There was grease everywhere. She not only put the syrup on the waffles but also on her chicken.

I ate half a waffle and couldn't eat anymore.

To cap it off, she started clipping her nails and left the shavings on the table. I didn't know if I should laugh or be revolted. We were eating at that table.

"So, what do you do?"

"I'm a stewardess," she said, her mouth open. I could see the chicken chewed up. I fought the urge to throw up.

"What do you do?"

I cleared my throat. My mom wasn't going to like it if I pulled the unemployment card. At least last time it had been inadvertent.

"I, um..." One of my clients said that I worked magic. "I'm a magician."

There was dead silence, not just at our table but throughout the entire restaurant.

"Like, for birthday parties?" She swallowed her food. "Okay."

"Hey! Entertainers do important work, you know. It's not like we would all be happy without entertainers." I was getting riled, and I wasn't even really a magician.

She took a drink of her water for the first time, instead of mutilating her meal. "That's okay, I guess. I don't know. I'm afraid of clowns."

I tilted my head a bit while I looked at her. "Clowns?"

"Yeah, they're just so creepy, you know?"

"Um, okay."

The conversation stuttered, then it faltered completely. We ate in complete silence for the rest of the meal, and I tried not to look at her chewed up food. I thought that both of us were relieved when I dropped her off at her house. She was quick to leave. It didn't look like being a magician was that impressive. It was just as effective as saying that I had the clap back when I was dating the woman who asked me how big our wedding should be five minutes into a first date.

I drove home. After this, I was going to flat-out

refuse all phone calls. I couldn't deal with my mom anymore or these crazy women she kept sending my way.

When I got home, I guessed that Jalanda had been waiting for me. There was a piece of chocolate cake out for me.

8 / CAKE
HUDSON

"AFTER THE LAST ONE, I thought that you might want this tonight."

"You thought right." I poured myself some bourbon, and I ate the chocolate cake. "This is sinfully good. Is this a new bakery or something?"

"It's mine." She suddenly looked shy and hunched her shoulders a little. "I am glad that you like it."

"You're a fantastic baker," I told her. "I'm so grateful that you made this for me."

"It was nothing. Just a little afternoon baking. By the way, Chris has to go for his shots soon."

"Really? He was just in the hospital."

"I booked an appointment for him at a pediatrician's office, but you need to come with me. I don't have your insurance information, and I don't have the ability to get all of Chris' medical needs taken care of since I'm not a parent."

"Okay." I finished my cake. "Can I have more?"

"Yes, of course." She took my plate, and she cut me another generous slice of cake. "How do you feel about chocolate cake a la mode?"

"Sounds fantastic."

She opened the refrigerator, and she took out a simple half gallon of vanilla ice cream. When she gave it back to me, the ice cream was melting a little bit on top of the cake. It was so cool to feel the cold sweetness. It made the chocolate just a tiny bit more bitter, and it was so good.

When I was done, I patted my stomach. "I'm so full. That was wonderful."

I stood up. "I want to look in on my son." No reason for her to know that my mother and I had creeped on her with Chris before. I looked into his room.

Like all babies, he was sound asleep. I looked at his breath rise and fall.

"He's so little." I said quietly. I didn't want to touch him. He might get hurt.

"You should hold him." Jalanda pulled him out of the crib, and she put him in my arms. I felt the soft, squishy weight of his body. I smelled the sweet smell of his hair. And for the first time, I understood why fathers cried when they held their children. How could I have stayed away from this miracle?

I felt ashamed that I had stayed away from my boy for so long. I didn't know what had come over me. Grief had been a part of it, sure, but this was my baby. Half of him was me. I kissed his cheek, and I put him back in his crib. He rolled over, trying to find me. I touched his petal-soft cheek, and he smiled.

"He smiled at me."

"Babies this young can't smile. He just...has a little gas or something."

"My son smiled at me."

Jalanda shrugged.

"Whatever you want."

I walked out of the room. Jalanda wasn't right behind me. She smoothed his hair a little bit, and then she walked out of the room, too.

"I'll see you bright and early tomorrow. The appointment is at 8 AM, so we're going to be battling worse traffic than usual. We should leave before 7:30."

I had been getting up around noon. I kept my groan to myself. "I'll be there. Good night."

I walked up the stairs and set an alarm. My evening had not turned out the way that I planned, but I definitely liked coming home to freshly baked, warm chocolate cake, especially with a scoop of ice cream on it. I tried to eat healthy, so the ice cream was never something that I would buy on my own. It was nice to have a woman's touch in the house.

I felt my heart drop. There were many woman's touches in the house. Isabel had stamped herself all over this space. I looked at her side of the bed with an embroidered pillow, and all the happiness from falling in love with my tiny son drained out of my body. The price of my child was the life of my wife.

I curled into a fetal ball on my bed. There would be no sleep tonight. I knew that some more bourbon would help, but it was unwise to let myself get dependent on alcohol to make me go to sleep.

9 / DOCTOR'S APPOINTMENT
JALANDA

I KNOCKED on his door at 7:25. "We have to leave in five minutes."

He came to the door. There were gigantic dark circles under his eyes.

"I'll be out in a minute."

He was out in a half minute. I looked him over. "I don't have time to give you coffee. I'll drive."

I already had Chris in a harness in a baby carrier, and his father was just as limp and tired as he was.

"You need sleep, you know. It's not like humans can exist without it."

His eyes shut. "I know that I need to sleep." That was it. That was all.

And so we drove in silence to the gray-white building where the doctor was. There were hundreds of doctors in that building. We needed to go to the fifth floor, according to the directory in the front of the building.

We walked into an elevator. I didn't want to carry Chris up 5 flights of stairs, no matter how sturdy the baby carrier was, and Hudson was in no shape to walk. He was red-eyed, and I knew that not all of that was from lack of sleep. He'd had a bit of bourbon when he came home, but he wasn't hungover. He was just sad.

I couldn't do anything about that, so I looked at Chris, snoozing away in his little nest of blankets.

When we got into the pediatrician's office, Hudson and I got all the paperwork on one of those clipboards with the pen attached to them with string. We sat down, and Hudson filled out all the necessary paperwork. I realized something was missing. I walked to the desk.

"Excuse me, do you have anything that would allow

me to act as Chris' guardian for medical purposes? I'm his nanny, and I don't want to bring his father every time."

"Oh, I thought you were his mom." I looked at my dark skin and at the pale as milk baby.

"Did you think he was adopted?"

She shrugged. "Yeah, of course we have the forms. Both of you need to sign them."

I brought them back to Hudson, who was halfway through filling out all the forms that he needed to fill out. We signed where the X signs were, and I gave everything back to the receptionist.

We didn't have long to wait. There was a nurse who came out to weigh the baby and take his vital signs. He was still asleep, and that made it easier to do what we needed to do.

He woke up when he heard another baby screaming in another one of the exam rooms. He started wailing just as loudly.

"Shh," I said, picking him up from his carrier. "Shh. It's okay."

He stopped crying, but he held out his little hands to his father. When he was this young, most of the world was pretty blurry. But somehow, he wanted his father to hold him.

Hudson looked at Chris.

"Do you want to hold him?"

Hudson hesitated for a half second. "Okay." He accepted Chris into his arms, and Chris stared up at his face with his wide, blue eyes.

The doctor came into the room. He checked every bit of Chris, which Chris did not like. No wonder the other baby had been crying earlier if going to the doctor was this uncomfortable.

"We need to give him his Hep B shot. I'll send someone in."

The doctor went out the door, and a nurse came in.

"Hold him still."

His father held one side, and I held the other. The nurse stuck a needle into Chris, and Chris let out a cry that nearly shattered my eardrums. I was pretty sure that a cry just a smidgen louder would be enough to wake the dead.

"And we're done. We'll charge you for the shot and for the exam today."

We went to the front, and Hudson paid whatever they asked for. We brought the carbon copy of the receipt home with us.

Chris was still fussy when we put him into the back seat of the car. I turned on the radio, hoping that the music would help. It did. He wasn't as upset. In the rearview mirror, I could see his face light up in a smile almost identical to his father's, if his father was drooling and had chubby, rosy cheeks.

When we got home, I put the receipt carefully into the folder where I kept all of the papers pertaining to Chris. I saw all the receipts.

"Oh, that reminds me. I need to show you to receipts for all of the stuff that I had to buy Chris."

Hudson waved me away. "Just keep it. I trust you. If I need to see it, I'll ask."

He was so casual about it, but I knew that having

his trust was a big deal. Something had happened with Hudson and Chris, and I could only pray that it would be a turn for the better. Chris and I spent all day every day together, and I cared for the baby just like he was my own baby. Chris deserved parents who loved him. With a dead mother, the only person that he had left was his father, who had been distant for the first few days of his life. Now that Hudson was beginning to bond with Chris, I hoped that they would have a real father-son relationship.

I went to brew some coffee. I heard steps coming down the stairs when the scent of coffee filled the kitchen.

"Smells good."

"I made enough for both of us."

When the coffee was ready, I poured a pot for the two of us.

"This is great coffee. What is it?"

"It's Colombian coffee. Do you take cream or sugar?"

10 / CEMETERY
HUDSON

AN OLD JOKE popped into my head. I like my coffee like I like my women. Strong and black. I didn't know where that came from, and I dismissed it from my mind. It had no place there. I couldn't touch the nanny. She was already becoming Chris' mother. I would not steal that from him lightly just so that I could feel her soft hands on my lonely body.

My phone rang, shaking me out of my head.

"Hello?"

"Hudson."

I knew that voice. It was Isabel's best friend, Mara.

"Hello, Mara."

"Hudson...I miss her so much." No preamble. She just got straight to it.

"I know." I gulped. "I do, too."

"Will you come with me to the cemetery? I bought flowers. I want to put them there."

"Yeah. I'll be right there as soon as I can."

I hung up the phone.

"Who was that?"

"Mara. She was my wife's best friend since childhood." I wiped my eye. Dust in it. "I am going to meet her at my wife's grave. Do you know where I can buy flowers?"

"There's a florist two blocks away. Just turn left when you get out of the neighborhood."

I normally had my secretary buy my wife flowers, and I had no idea where they came from. But my wife, my secretary, and my company were gone now. I just had numbers in my bank account.

I stopped and bought her a bouquet of pink calla lilies. They were her favorite, the kind that I bought for Valentine's Day and her birthday.

I drove to the cemetery. My vision was a little blurry from the tears, but I knew that it would be fine.

I parked my car a little bit off of the roadway. There was a one-lane road that went all through the cemetery, and only one car could get through at a time. I tried not to be in anybody's way.

Mara was already there at the grave. She had pink calla lilies in a little vase in front of the grave.

"Hudson. You're here."

I could see that her nose was pink, and her eyes were red. She had been crying. She had a scarf with wet spots on it.

"Mara." I opened my arms, and she stepped into them.

"I miss her so much!" she whispered into my ear. "I miss her like you wouldn't believe."

"I know. I do, too." I was ashamed that I had believed that my grief was overwhelming, that it made me think that I was the only person in the world. I wasn't the only person who had lost Isabel. Mara had known Isabel almost her entire life, and the shock of having someone so close to you die had to sting almost as much as losing my wife.

"She's somewhere better now."

"I'm sorry for crying all over you," she whispered. "I just haven't been able to wrap my head around it."

I looked down at her crying face right next to mine. Her eyes went huge as I went in and kissed her mouth.

I sprang back as if she'd suddenly burst into flame.

"Oh my god. I am so sorry. I have no idea what got into me."

"It's okay!" She blinked. "Um, wow. What?"

"My mom has been setting me up with a ton of insane women. I just...I don't know...I haven't been sleeping well. That's no excuse. I'm sorry."

"Do you want to go on a date?"

I was just as shocked as she had been when I kissed her.

"You're asking me out?" Was this a Sadie Hawkins dance?

"Yeah. Why not? I am not dating anybody, and your mother is already pushing you towards dating people. I bet you can fool her by dating me."

I thought about it. Mom wouldn't rest until she felt like I had crawled out of my cave.

"Okay. Let's do dinner tonight."

"I'll cook." Mara smiled, even though her eyes were still puffy. "I'll make you my world-famous spaghetti and meatballs."

"World-famous, huh? Sounds good." I smiled. Isabel had always stolen Mara's recipes, so I was pretty sure that I'd had her 'world-famous' spaghetti and meatballs before. "What time?"

"Let's say 8. I'll drop by the store and get things set up."

"Sounds good. I'll bring some wine." I kept a bunch of Bordeaux in a wine cooler, since I didn't have a wine cellar in my house. I felt slightly guilty that I didn't drink California wine, but it just wasn't as good as French wine.

"Perfect. I'll see you then." She got into her little Jag and drove off.

I watched her. And I looked back at the bright pink calla lilies on my dead wife's grave. I hope you would be okay with this.

I drove home. I called my mom.

11 / MARA'S DATE
HUDSON

"Mom, guess what?" I told her before she could even say hello. "I'm dating someone."

"Oh, really? Is it that second girl?"

"No, Mom. It's Mara. You remember her, Isabel's maid of honor."

Mom was quiet. I wondered if the line was cut off. "Mom? Are you there?"

"Yes, yes, I'm here." She cleared her throat. "Well, I hope that you are happy with her. There's no reason for you to rush into a relationship so soon after your wife's death."

This woman had set me up with two women immediately after my wife died. She was unbelievable. "Okay, Mom." Whatever. "I have to go."

I went to the nursery to check on Jalanda and Chris. She had Chris in her lap, and he was trying to tear the pages out of the sturdy cardboard book.

"I'm going to be in late tonight."

"Got another disastrous date?"

"No, I'm going out with Mara. Well, in. She's cooking me spaghetti."

"Oh, okay. Have fun. Chris and I will have a quiet night. No worries."

Did I imagine it, or did she looked worried about me and a little jealous? I shook off the thought. I'd hired her to take care of my son and keep the household running, with groceries always in the fridge. Jalanda fit into my life like a puzzle piece. It was a relief not to have to keep track of when the cleaning service came, and the dishes were always washed. In college, I'd let them sit in the sink for days at a time.

I walked upstairs to think about what I should bring to Mara's house. I'd bring the wine I had promised, of course, but I should bring flowers, as well. What would be appropriate for your first date with your wife's best friend?

I decided on yellow roses. They said hello, but they didn't say that I wanted to rip her clothes off. It was funny, because she looked so much like Isabel, but I had never thought of her that way. She was just Mara to me. That night with Mara was the first time that I felt alive since Isabel died. We joked, and we laughed. We looked at pictures of Isabel. It didn't hurt as much to look at them. I knew that she had been happy with me. We'd been so good for each other. I'd pinned her down, gotten her to be on time. She'd made me try new things. I was a better man with her, and that would never change.

She also would have made me live, just like my mom did. I was only twenty-two, despite building my business since I was 15, and I knew that she would want more from me than crumpling into a ball of sadness.

I began to spend every night at Mara's house. I told Jalanda not to wait up for me. That night with the chocolate cake had been good, but she needed to rest so that she could take care of my tiny son. I stopped in every morning to just roll around on the carpet with him. He was getting just a little bigger and a little heavier every day. I thought that he'd grow taller than my own six feet. His body was so long for a baby, and he'd been 10 pounds and 6 ounces when he was born. He probably had some big bones to hold up a frame like mine.

I would help bathe him before I went out for dinner. His favorite time of the day was splashing me with water. I learned quickly not to wear anything but swim trunks with my boy around. Water was his element.

It was three months before Mara changed the game.

"My lease is going to end soon."

"Oh." I ate some more of the chicken parmigiana she had cooked. "Is that so?"

"Yes. You know, you have a pretty big house. I remember when you two were looking at it. You have tons of empty bedrooms."

"Yeah. We do." I got where she was going, but I wasn't going to help her get there.

"You're over here every night anyways. What if I moved in with you? You could spend more time with Chris."

I sat back and thought about it. I had more bedrooms than anybody could ever need. For some reason, I wanted a big house. Isabel had wanted something smaller. It was hard-coded in me that a big house meant that you made it. I wished that I had complied with what Isabel had wanted while she was alive.

"Okay." I had nobody else to run it by. "You know that my son and my nanny already live with me, right?"

"Of course," Mara said, her perfect white teeth revealed in a lovely smile that dazzled me a little bit. "They'll hardly notice me."

12 / MARA MOVES IN
JALANDA

MARA HAD a moving van bring her stuff into Hudson's house. It was a good thing that Hudson had so much space; otherwise, the quantity of stuff that came in would have been overwhelming. She brought her own chairs, tables, a couch, and just a ton of furniture. We crammed it in everywhere that it would go. Hudson helped the movers. Mara had to have everything just so.

I retreated even more deeply into the nursery. Mara cooked all of our meals, and I would get the leftovers and eat while Chris had his bottle. I saw less of Hudson now that Mara lived in our house.

I lived on the basement level that was halfway above ground. I had my own parking spot, and I had my own entrance. One day, when I was coming home with more formula and diapers for Chris — I only fed him more to make more come out — I heard a conversation between Mara and someone else. She was on the house phone.

"Yeah, I have to live here now."

"No, I can't go."

"NO! I have to stay here until he proposes, at least."

The other person had a lot to say about that. "I can't help that."

"Don't you want to be a millionaire?"

My blood ran cold. "You know he's loaded with that IT business. He didn't sign a prenup with Isabel, and I doubt that he would sign one with me. It's easy money. Free."

I put my hand over my mouth. Unless my ears were completely wrong, Mara was planning to take all of Hudson's money.

That night, Mara went off to a ballet class, and I had dinner with Hudson alone for the first time since she came.

We sat down to spaghetti with arrabbiata sauce

"Hudson. I have to talk to you about something."

His ears perked up. "Is it your salary? I'll double it to keep you here."

"No. It's about Mara. You know how you went out to the club to play some tennis today?"

He nodded. "I went to the grocery store, and Mara didn't know that I came home." I sighed. "I overheard something that was kind of weird."

"What was it?"

"She was saying that she wanted to marry you without a prenup and take money from the sale of your business."

His face contorted with anger. "What a vicious lie."

I felt as if he had slapped me across the face. "I'm not lying. I really did hear her. She didn't hear me come in, because my part of the house has a separate entrance."

His voice could have frozen ice in the Sahara. "You don't need to work here. Mara is an angel, just like my Isabel was. I'll give you severance or whatever, but you won't look after my son for another minute.

I don't want you to be in this house in an hour. Pack your things and go."

Tears streamed down my face. I packed my suitcase. I had only been living here for a few months, but it felt like my home. I looked at Chris sleeping in his crib, which I wheeled to the doorway of his nursery so I could watch him during dinner. He was practically my own baby. We spent all of our time together. I leaned over and kissed his delicate little cheek. He shifted in his sleep, as if he knew that this was his mama, saying goodbye.

I saw one of my tears drop onto his blanket, making a little wet splotch.

Hudson was standing at the door, his mouth in a firm line, his blue eyes stormy just like a hurricane.

"Bye." I nodded to him. "You can send my severance to the nanny agency." They'd take a cut, but I didn't want to talk to this man again.

I put my things into my car and tried not to cry, but the tears came down anyway. My baby was gone. Not dead. Just gone. All for the sake of that darned gold-digger.

13 / ANOTHER VISIT
HUDSON

MY MOTHER SHOWED up unexpectedly again. I swore, she was just like a tumbleweed, rolling into town and just rolling straight out again.

She went straight for the nursery when she arrived. Chris was crying, just as he had cried every day and night since Jalanda left.

"Where's the girl? Why is my grandson crying?"

"I fired her." I couldn't meet my mother's eyes. I stared at the floor, feeling like I was a recalcitrant teenager.

"You fired her? Why?"

"She told me a lie about Mara."

My mom put a finger under my chin and made me meet her eyes. "What lie?"

"She said that Mara was trying to marry me for my money. She said that Mara wanted to be pre-nup free. It was ridiculous. I'm so far away from trying to marry anybody anytime soon. Mara and I are just having fun."

My mom paused. "I see."

"Do you? Because I've been questioning that decision every day since then. I've already gone through three nannies in the last week. They tell me that they can't handle Chris' colic. It's not colic. He didn't scream like that when Jalanda was here."

My mother rubbed an eyebrow. "Yes, of course he didn't. Why don't you hire her back?"

"I can't get in touch with her. I checked with the nanny agency, but they won't give me her personal contact information. They said that it's a violation of her privacy. I have a private investigator looking for her, but that's going to take time. I have no idea where she's gotten to."

My mom drummed her fingers on the table lightly. "I see what you mean. I'll see what I can do."

"Chris wants her back. He can't even talk yet, but I know."

"You want her back." My mother wasn't asking me a question.

"Of course. She's the only one who can stop Chris from crying morning and night. Mara says that she has a migraine from the baby. She wants me to put him in daycare."

My mother sucked in a breath. "Do you want to?"

"No, of course not. I'm at home. It doesn't make any sense to send my son away. He's too young. I'll put him in preschool when the time comes, but daycare when he's only a few months old is nonsensical."

"Good." My mother stood up. "I'll look into finding Jalanda. Tell your private investigator to call me and tell me what he's gotten so far. I have some suspicions, but I'm really not sure where she could have gone. Goodbye, Hudson."

And just like that, my mother swept out.

I sighed.

Today's nanny came out, her eyes red. She had been crying just like my son.

"I can't take it anymore. He's like a demon baby. He's never happy. He's the worst child I've ever looked after. He just screams for temper. I've fed him. I've rocked him. He just fights everything and screams louder."

That did not sound like my little baby.

"Just pay the agency for a half day. I'm done here."

She took her bag and left. My son was left alone with me and Mara.

Mara came home just five minutes after Mom left. She found me holding a screaming baby. I frankly was impressed by Chris' lung capacity. If I had screamed for that loud and that long, I would have passed out, but he was still going strong.

"What happened? Where is your nanny?"

"She quit, just like the rest of them. No one can handle this baby. Do you want to try?"

She looked at Chris' wretched, red little face and

the snot and drool coming out of his little nose and mouth.

"No, thank you. When does your next nanny arrive?"

"I'm not getting another nanny. Nobody wants to stay with my son. I'm going to take care of my son myself."

"I don't think that's a wise decision." Mara closed her eyes. "I mean, shouldn't he be taken care of by someone who knows what they are doing?"

"He's been taken care of by several someones who knew what they were doing. He doesn't want them. He wants somebody in particular, and I can't find her."

"Well, I'm not staying here with that baby screaming his head off every second of the day. I'll be back after he's gone to sleep." Mara walked right back out the door.

Isabel would never have done that.

My house was wired with security cameras. It was something that we did for some of the small businesses, and manufacturers would send test units to me sometimes, hoping to convince me to buy their cameras for my clients. I had them rigged all around the house.

I went to review the tape from when I had my tennis game. My calendar told me the time and date that I was gone.

My 16 screens told me the story. There was Jalanda's car pulling into the driveway. There was Mara talking on my phone. I played back the audio for that screen.

My mouth dropped when I heard what Mara was saying. I had no idea who she had on the phone, but Jalanda had been telling the absolute truth. Mara was in it to win it. She wanted my money. That explained why we hadn't kissed since that day in the cemetery.

14 / TEA
JALANDA

"More tea, sweetheart?"

I was sitting on the front porch of Mrs. King's log cabin. To call it a cabin was a massive understatement. It was a very large house built in the woods.

I had gone for a very long camping trip to clear my head after Hudson fired me for telling the truth about Mara. I should have just kept it to myself. Just because I kept myself to strict standards of integrity didn't mean that the rest of the world did. I wasn't too old to already know about that. People lied all the time. And really, was wanting money so terrible? Mara had just wanted some material goods.

I wanted Chris back. That first night, I had wildly thought up a scheme to steal him away with me. I'd set up a whole new life with us far away in Canada. Hudson barely bothered with Chris for the first week of his life. Maybe he didn't need a father. He'd have all the love he needed in me.

But I knew that it would be wrong to separate the two of them. Hudson had fallen in love with Chris, and they belonged together. They had the same stubborn streak.

You might think that just because Chris couldn't talk yet, he would be hard to understand. Chris and I understood each other very well. I may have given him his baths, fed him food, and clothed him, but he wanted things the way that he wanted. I smiled when I thought about the way that he had wiggled when I put him in the onesie that he despised. It was green instead of blue like all of his other clothes. For some reason, he absolutely hated it. But after he spit up on a different onesie, it was the only one we had while I put his things into the wash. He had squirmed and wiggled until his legs were in the arm holes. I had to take him out, and he'd ended up going naked while the laundry was washed and dried.

I would never hold his squirming little body again. I felt a sense of loss as I thought about another nanny coming in and replacing me. Chris might remember me for right now, but as he grew up, he'd forget me. And I loved him like he was my own.

Mrs. King had found my camping spot, and she had insisted that I stay in her cabin. Mansion. Whatever. I was grateful for a hot shower, so I didn't protest too much. She had given me my own room, one that was substantially more bug-free than my tent was.

"Yes, I'd love some more. I've been eating dried food and trail mix out here."

Mrs. King shook her head. "My son is looking for you, you know."

"Is he? He fired me. I didn't think that he cared."

"He does. He may not have told you, but he does."

I blinked. What was she talking about? "What do you mean?"

"I can see it in his face. He does care about you, but he has no idea how to express himself. So he's just twiddling his thumbs, totally lost with a baby who hasn't stopped crying since you left, living with that wretched gold-digger."

"You believe me?" I hadn't even told her. "Why?"

She shook her head. "I knew about her from day one. I watched as she flirted with all of the most expensively dressed men at Hudson's wedding. That woman is the most conniving female I've met in my life, and I've met quite a few."

I shook my head. "That's so flattering, but I don't want Hudson to know where I am. He fired me. I should be telling the agency to find me another position, but I haven't."

"You shouldn't. Come work for me."

I was taken aback. I blinked again and again. "What?"

"Work for me. I don't need a nanny, but I can make you my personal assistant. I certainly need one of those to keep my life on track."

Hudson had been a very generous employer, but I could not exist out here in the woods forever. Mrs. King seemed kind, and maybe I'd get to see Chris again. I'd do it for a little while at least.

"Okay."

15 / CABIN
HUDSON

I DROVE down the long dirt road to my mother's cabin. She'd insisted on having it as a retreat from my dad's business interests. They went out on the weekends. My dad worked hard, and they spent a lot of time together, just the two of them, out here. During the summer, the whole family would come out and stay here, with Dad commuting back to the city for the workweek. It brought back memories when I smelled the earthy scent of the forest. I liked it a lot. I should get out here more often. It wasn't like Mother had the time to get out here. Without Dad, she was a woman alone deep in the woods. She had two double-barreled shotguns in a gun cage, but I didn't feel right about having her out here all by herself.

When I got to the cabin, I could see Mother bustling around the kitchen. Back home, she let the domestic staff do all of the work. When she brought my father out here, she cared for him all by herself. He wasn't kept to the standard that he kept in our home, but it was nice for us to be alone for once. What happened in the family was never private, because we had people who lived with us. Our servants, over time, became part of the family, but they were not related to us by blood.

I parked my car in the grass, and I put my sunglasses away in my car. I didn't need them inside of the cabin.

With my Gucci sunglasses gone, I looked nothing like the person that I was in Los Angeles. Staring into the side mirror, I looked insanely young. I had shaved off my beard when I kicked Mara out. I touched the smooth skin, with hair threatening to break the surface already. Mara had been a terrible decision.

But I couldn't find Jalanda to make it up to her.

I took Chris out of his carseat. The motion of the car made him sleep and stop crying. He had stopped screaming all the time, but it made me sad. His spirit was broken by Jalanda's departure and subsequent absence.

I walked into the cabin, and I smelled something delightful.

"Is that bacon? Hello, Mom."

My mother was wearing an apron, looking like the picture of Suzy Homemaker and not the terrifying society doyenne who ran things her way with an iron fist. For some reason, seeing her like this just made me more scared of her. She was a wolf in sheep's clothing.

"Hello, Hudson." She kissed the air next to my cheek, careful not to mess up her makeup. "I have a surprise for you."

"Is it two pounds of bacon? I'm starving, and I better eat something before the baby wakes up. He's been so sad since Jalanda left."

"I'll put Chris on one of the beds. There's someone here I want you to meet."

With dread, I watched her pick up my son and take him away. What fresh hell was this? I didn't want to meet anybody. I knew the only person that I wanted to have in my home.

Like a vision, she appeared in the doorway. She was taking off her muddy hiking boots.

"MRS. KING, I gathered the mushrooms you wanted for dinner." Beside her was a basket filled with mushrooms still covered in dirt. She had a small shovel in it.

"Jalanda!" I got to my feet.

"What are you doing here?"

She looked like she regretted taking off her boots. She looked at them, mentally calculating how long it would take to put them on and run.

"Your mother hired me as her personal assistant. She wants me to help her out, and that's the best term we had for it."

"You can't work for my mother. You work for me."

She crossed her arms and snapped her fingers.

"No, sir. You fired me."

"Jalanda, I want you to come back. Chris has missed you so much. He cried constantly for a week after you left, and now he's depressed."

"How can a baby be depressed?"

Good question. "Because he cries a lot?" I wasn't sure.

"Are you asking me to come back because of Chris or because of you?"

I knew the answer, and I might as well tell the truth. I got to one knee.

"Jalanda, will you do me the honor of becoming my wife?"

Her hand went to her throat. "Oh my god."

"I don't have a ring. I had no idea that you were here. But I will get one as soon as possible."

She tugged my arm. "Get up. I don't want to get married to you."

"I'm staying right here in this cabin until you do."

She snorted. "You're going to get pretty tired of me, then."

"Why don't you want to marry me?" There were a lot of women who would love to marry a multimillionaire.

"For one thing, we've never dated. We've never even kissed."

"I could fix that right now," I offered.

For the first time since I came, I saw her smile. "For the second, you fired me because I told you the truth about your girlfriend."

"I need to apologize about that. I ran back my security tapes for the day that you told me about. I heard her talking on the phone, too. I should have trusted you."

"Yes, you should have."

"I promise that I'll spend the rest of my life making it up to you. I promise to have faith in you and trust you until the day I die. You fill my life with light where before I only saw darkness. I love you, Sunshine."

Her eyes were filled with tears. "Do you mean that?"

"Yes."

Her tears fell to her cheeks.

I stood up and kissed the salty tears. I kissed her adorable nose. Then I kissed her mouth, which tasted so sweet, like the best candy in the world, better than anything that Willy Wonka could concoct.

"Say yes," I whispered. "I will treat you like a princess from now on. I promise."

She looked up at me. Our eyes met. She saw the sincerity shining through.

"I'll marry you."

I heard the sound of clapping from the corner of the room. My mother was standing there.

"Finally. Honestly, you two, you're so hard-headed."

We heard the sounds of Chris waking up alone. He started to scream.

Jalanda ran to the bedroom. The instant that she

walked in, Chris stopped. I could see the curve of her luscious form as she bent over to pick him up out of the nest of pillows on the bed. She put him in the spot where she always carried him, and Chris drooled all over her, complete bliss on his face.

I smiled. The two of them were my little family, and I wouldn't trade it for anything in the world.

EPILOGUE
JALANDA

MY WEDDING DRESS felt too tight all through our wedding day, but I was so happy to finally marry Hudson that I barely noticed. His mother, like always, swept in to arrange his second marriage in as many years without getting a single hair out of place. When I grew up, I wanted to be her.

I needed the help, as much as I didn't want to admit it. She was the only one that knew my secret, the one that I had been keeping from Hudson as he got increasingly scared that I was going to back out of our wedding. No matter how many times I tried to soothe him, he woke up from nightmares that I had left him, that I had died just like his first wife had.

It wouldn't help to tell him about my pregnancy. It

was the exact same thing that had stolen Isabel, and he would be an absolute basket case if he knew during the wedding.

I tried not to cry tears of joy when the pair of us stood in front of the celebrant and all of our friends and family as we pledged to spend the rest of our lives together, to cherish one another no matter what the years brought.

He had promised me that he would be a better man, with more faith and trust. The first thing that I had done in the house was move all of Isabel's handmade things into the nursery. While Chris would never know his mother, he could at least see who she had been and what she had done. I turned one of his walls into a mural of Hudson holding hands with Isabel, so that Chris would grow up with an image of pure love.

As Chris started to talk, he said the words mum-mum first. Everyone likes to think that those words mean Mother, but it's really the first sounds that a baby is capable of making and it usually indicates that said baby is hungry. I knew to feed Chris a bottle when he started babbling.

He'd grown so fast that it was incredible. I'd had to buy new clothes for him what felt like every day. When I pushed him around in a stroller, people asked me, "Isn't he too old for a stroller?" He looked much older than he really was. I knew he'd grow to be a big, strong man like his daddy.

Inside of my stomach was a tiny peanut. I hadn't gotten an ultrasound yet, but a blood test had shown me a precious baby. I had no idea if it was a boy or girl, but it didn't matter. As long as the baby was healthy, I would be happy.

At the end of the night, after we'd walked around and been forced to kiss time and time again by forks clanging on glasses, Hudson picked me up and took me away from the raucous rejoicing of our mutual families.

"You didn't drink any alcohol tonight. How will I be able to convince you to have my wicked way with you?"

I meant to tell him later, after the honeymoon, but somehow the moment was coming now, too early.

"Hudson, there's a reason why I didn't drink."

"Oh? Were you a closet alcoholic or something? The Italian wines were too much?"

"No." I shook my head. "I'm pregnant."

All of my fears melted away when he kissed me long, deep, and wet.

"That's the best news I've heard all day."

He put his hand on my stomach. "I can't wait to meet our baby."

THE END